KODANSHA NIHONGO FOLKTALES SERIES 1

ももたろう

MOMOTARO, THE PEACH BOY

SHA INTERNATIONAL
o·New York·London

おじいさん「いってきます」
おばあさん「いっていらっしゃい。おじいさん、
きを　つけて」
　おばあさん　は　かわ　へ　せんたく　に
いきました。そして、おおきな　もも　を
みつけました。
おばあさん「あっ、おおきな　もも！
おいしそう！　おじいさん　と　たべ
ましょう」
　おばあさん　は　その　もも　を　うち
へ　もって　かえりました。
おじいさん「ただいま」
おばあさん「おかえりなさい」
おじいさん「あっ、おおきな
もも　だ　なあ。おいしそう！」
おばあさん「さあ、たべましょう」

かわ
もも

おばあさん　が、その　もも　を　ほうちょう
で　きりました。すると、もも　の　なか
から　おおきい　げんきな　あかちゃん　が
とびだしました。
ももたろう「いち、に、さん！　こんにちは
おじいさん！　こんにちは　おばあさん！
ぼく　の　なまえ　は　ももたろう　です。

どうぞ　よろしく」
ももたろう　は　おおきな
こえ　で　いいました。
おじいさん　も
おばあさん　も　びっくり
しました。

おじいさん「かわいい
あかちゃん　だ」
おばあさん「じょうぶな
あかちゃん　だ。おにぎり
を　たくさん　たべなさい」
おじいさん　と　おばあ
さん　は　ももたろう　を
だいじに　そだてました。
ももたろう　は　げんき
で　やさしい　こども
でした。おじいさん　や
おばあさん　の　しごと
を　てつだいました。

そして　おじいさん　と　おばあ
さん　の　せわ　を　しました。
ももたろう「おじいさん　おつかれさま。
かた　を　たたきましょう」
おじいさん「ありがとう」

ももたろう「おばあさん　おつかれさま。あし　を　もみましょう」

おばあさん「ありがとう」

ももたろう　は　やさしい　こども　でした。そして　たいへん　ちからもち　でした。いつも　むらのひとたち　の　しごと　を　てつだいました。

ももたろう「いち、に、さん、よいしょ」

むらのひと1「ありがとう」

むらのひと2「ももたろうさん　は　とても　やさしい　ね」

むらのひと3「ももたろうさん　は　ちからもち　だね」

おにがしま　に　わるい　おに　が
たくさん　すんで　いました。ときどき
むら　へ　きて　おこめ　や　おかね
や　たからもの　を　とって　いき
ました。むらのひとたち　は　たいへん
こまって　いました。

おに　の　おやぶん　「むら　へ　いって
おこめ　を　とって　こい」
あかおに　「はい」
おに　の　おやぶん　「むら　へ　いって
おかね　を　とって　こい」

あおおに　「はい」
おに　の　おやぶん　「むら　へ　いって
たからもの　を　とって　こい。ぜんぶ
とって　こい」
おじいさん　「ああ、こまった！　こまっ
た！　また　わるい　おに　が　きた」

おばあさん　「うち　の　おこめ
も　おさけ　も　みんなとって
いった。どうしよう」
ももたろう　「じゃあ、ぼく
が　おにがしま　へ　いって
おに　を　みんな　たいじ
しよう」
おばあさん　「あぶない　から
いかないで」
ももたろう　「だいじょうぶ、
だいじょうぶ」
おじいさん　も　おばあさん
も　ももたろう　の　おに
たいじ　が　しんぱい　でした。

ももたろう「おばあさん、にっぽんいち の
きびだんご を つくって ください」
おばあさん「はいはい たくさん つくり
ましょう」
おじいさん「この かたな を もって
いきなさい」
ももたろう「ありがとう。では、いって
まいります」
ももたろう は はちまき を しめて、

かたな を こし に さし、
にっぽんいち の きびだんご
を もって、おにたいじ に
でかけました。
ももたろう は ひとり で
げんきに やまみち を あるいて
いきました。
とちゅうで いっぴき の いぬ に
あいました。

はちまき
きびだんご
かたな

ももたろう
いぬ

いぬ　「ももたろうさん、ももたろうさん、
どこ　へ　いくんですか」
ももたろう　「おにがしま　へ　おにたいじ
に　いくの　だよ」
いぬ　「それは　なんです　か」
ももたろう　「にっぽんいち　の　きびだんご　だよ」
いぬ　「ひとつ　ください。いっしょに
いって、おに　を　やっつけましょう」
ももたろう　「うん、いいよ。はい、ひとつ
あげましょう」
いぬ　は　きびだんご　を　もらって
ももたろう　の　けらい　に　なりました。

ももたろう と いぬ は やま の なか で さる に あいました。
さる 「ももたろうさん、ももたろうさん、どこ へ いくんです か」
ももたろう 「おにがしま へ おにたいじ に」
さる 「それ は なんです か」
ももたろう 「にっぽんいち の きびだんご だよ」
さる 「ひとつ ください。いっしょに いって おに を やっつけましょう」
ももたろう 「うん、いいよ。はい、ひとつ」
さる も きびだんご を もらって、ももたろう の けらい に なりました。

ももたろう と いぬ と さる は もり の なか で きじ に あいました。

きじ「ももたろうさん、どこ へ いくんです か」
ももたろう「おにがしま へ」
きじ「それ は なんです か」
ももたろう「にっぽんいち の きびだんご だよ」
きじ「ひとつ ください。いっしょに いって、おに を やっつけましょう」
ももたろう「うん、いいよ」
きじ も ももたろう の けらい に なりました。

ももたろう は いぬ と さる と きじ と いっしょに うみへ いって、みんな で ふね に のりました。やがて、とおくに おにがしま が みえました。

ももたろう 「さあ、おにがしま に ついたよ。みんな がんばろう！」

いぬ さる きじ 「がんばろう！」

ももたろう と いぬ と さる と きじ は ふね から おりて、いわ の うえ を あるいて いきました。

おに の おしろ の おおきな てつ の もん の まえ まで きました。

ももたろう 「なか から もん を あけなさい」

さる 「はい、わかりました」

ももたろう 「さあ、みんな なか へ すすめ！」

ももたろう と いぬ と さる と きじ は おしろ の なか へ はいって いきました。

もん
ももたろう

ももたろう

おしろ　の　なか　では、おにたち　が
おさけ　を　のんだり、ごちそう　を　たべたり、
うた　を　うたったり　おどり　を　おどったり、
おおさわぎ　を　していました。
おにのおやぶん　「さあ、たくさん　のめ
のめ。うたえ、うたえ。おどれ、おどれ！」
あかおに　「もう、おなか　が　いっぱい　だ」
あおおに　「もう、よっぱらった」
ももたろう　は　かたな　を　ぬいて　へや　の
なか　に　とびこみました。
おにたち　は　おどろいて、おおきな　かなぼう
を　ふりまわしました。

おにのおやぶん　「おまえ　は　だれだ」

ももたろう　「ぼく　は　にっぽんいち　の　ももたろうだ！」

おにのおやぶん　「かえれ、かえれ。この　かなぼう　で　やっつける　ぞ！」

ももたろう　「むらのひとたち　の　たからもの　を　かえしなさい」

いぬ　「おに　の　あし　に　かみつこう」

さる「おに の かお
を ひっかこう」
きじ「おに の あたま
を つっつこう」
ももたろう たち は
にっぽんいち の
きびだんご を
たべた ので
げんきです。

おにのおやぶん　「ごめんなさい。たからもの
は　ぜんぶ　かえします」
あかおに　あおおに　「もう　わるい　こと　は
しません。どうぞ　ゆるして　ください」
おにたち　は　ないて　あやまりました。
ももたろう　は　たからもの　を　くるま
に　のせて　むら　へ　かえって　きました。
むらのひとたち　「あ、ももたろうさん　が
かえってきた。ばんざい、ばんざい」
ももたろう　「ただいま、かえりました」
おじいさん　「おかえり。よかった、よかった」
おばあさん　「おかえりなさい。ごくろうさま」
むらのひとたち　「ありがとう。ももたろうさん
は　ほんとうに　にっぽんいち　だ」

ももたろう
くるま

p. 18
がんばろう
Let's do our best, let's go for it.

おしろ
Castle.

すすめ
Forward! Advance!

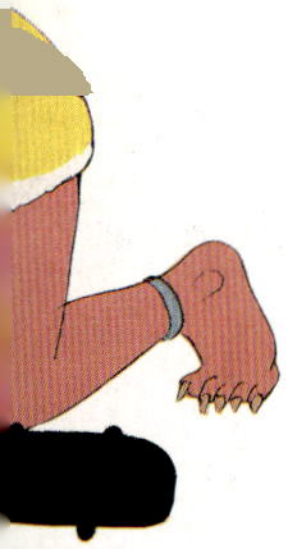

p. 21
かなぼう
Spiked metal clubs. The expression **おに に かなぼう** means "the demons are powerful, almost unbeatable." So when the demons threaten Momotaro with their clubs it sounds like a battle Momotaro cannot possibly win.

p. 22
おまえ
You. There are many words for "you" in Japanese—this one is used by men, and is impolite.

かみつこう
I'll bite.

p. 23
ひっかこう
I'll scratch.

つっつこう
I'll peck.

p. 24
ごめんなさい
I'm sorry, we're sorry. This is a polite way to say "sorry" in Japanese.

ばんざい
Hooray! This is what people say when they cheer in Japan, for example, when someone wins a sporting championship. Literally, it means "ten thousand years," that is, you hope the person you are cheering will live forever. However, Japanese people do not think too much about the meaning when they are busy cheering!

ごくろうさま
Thank you for your efforts. This is a way of saying thanks to someone who has just done a particularly difficult job.

だいじょうぶ
Okay, alright.

おにたいじ
Subdue the demons. From おに, demon, and たいじ, subdue.

p. 12

にっぽんいち
The best in Japan.

きびだんご
Millet dumplings. きびだんご were originally dumplings made of ground millet, but the きびだんご commonly available now in Japan tend to be made of a kind of sticky rice instead, and are smaller than the original ones.

はちまき
A kind of headband tied round the forehead, mainly by men when they are going to do some kind of hard work.

いぬ
Dog.

p. 15

けらい
Follower, retainer. This word was used in feudal Japan to mean the follower of a feudal lord.

p. 16

さる
Monkey.

p. 17

きじ
Pheasant.

おつかれさま
You must be tired. A common phrase in Japanese, often said to someone who has just finished a day's work.

ありがとう
Thank you. There are many ways of saying "thank you" in Japanese. This is one of the simplest and most generally useful.

p. 9

ちからもち
Strong. Literally, strong person

よいしょ
There you go. You can say this when you are doing something that takes physical effort, for example, lifting something heavy.

p. 10

おにがしま
Demon Island. From **おに**, demon, and **しま**, island.

おに
A large demon, about seven feet tall, with horns and big teeth. They are mischievous and like playing tricks on human beings, but are not usually thought of as very frightening.

おやぶん
Chief, boss.

あかおに
Red demon. From **あか**, red, and **おに**, demon.

p. 11

あおおに
Blue demon, from **あお**, blue, and **おに**, demon.

おさけ
Sake, Japanese rice wine.

たいじしよう
I'll subdue.

p. 4

おじいさん
Grandfather. Also has the wider meaning of "old man"—any old man, not just your own grandfather.

いってきます
I'm going out now. This is what Japanese people say when they leave home for a short time, for example, to go to work or to go shopping. You only say it when you leave your own home, not when you leave someone else's home.

おばあさん
Grandmother. Similar to **おじいさん**, **おばあさん** has a wider meaning of "old woman."

いって　いらっしゃい
See you soon. This is a response to **いってきます**. If you are staying at home, you say it to anyone else in your family who is going out. It literally means "You are going out," but in English we would simply say "Goodbye."

もも
Peach.

ただいま
I'm home, I'm back. This is what Japanese people say when they return home, for example, after a day's work or a shopping trip.

おかえりなさい
Welcome back. This is the response to **ただいま**—Japanese people say it to welcome other members of the family home.

p. 7

げんき
Healthy, lively, or full of energy.

こんにちは
An expression of greeting used from about midday until the evening. (Different greetings are used in the morning and evening.)

p. 8

おにぎり
Rice balls that have various different savoury fillings. Popular as a snack or packed lunch in Japan—the traditional Japanese equivalent of sandwiches.

p. 16

In the mountains, Momotaro and the dog met a monkey.
Monkey: "Momotaro, Momotaro, where are you going?"
Momotaro: "I'm going to Onigashima to subdue the demons."
Monkey: "What's that you've got there?"
Momotaro: "These are the best millet dumplings in the whole of Japan."
Monkey: "Give me one and we'll go attack the demons together."
Momotaro: "OK, here you are, have one."

p. 17

So the monkey, too, got one of the millet dumplings, and became Momotaro's faithful follower.
In the woods, Momotaro, the dog, and the monkey met a pheasant.
Pheasant: "Momotaro, where are you going?"
Momotaro: "I'm going to Onigashima."
Pheasant: "What's that you've got there?"
Momotaro: "These are the best millet dumplings in the whole of Japan."
Pheasant: "Give me one and we'll go attack the demons together."
Momotaro: "OK, here you are."
So the pheasant, too, became Momotaro's faithful follower.

p. 18

Momotaro, the dog, the monkey, and the pheasant all went together to the sea, and got on a boat. After a while they could see Onigashima in the distance.
Pheasant: "I can see Onigashima!"
Monkey: "I can see it!" I can see it!"
Dog: "I can see it! I can see it!"
Momotaro: "Well, here we are in Onigashima. Let's go for it!"
Dog, Monkey, Pheasant: "Go for it!"
Momotaro, the dog, the monkey, and the pheasant got out of the boat and set off across the rocks. They came to the front of the huge iron gate of the demon's castle.
Momotaro: "Go open the gate from the inside."
Monkey: "OK, I've got it."
Momotaro: "Well, everyone, forward into the castle!"
Momotaro, the dog, the monkey, and the pheasant went into the castle.

p. 21

The inside of the castle was in uproar, as the demons drank *sake*, ate their fill, sang songs, and danced.
Chief demon: "Drink as much as you like. Sing, sing. Dance, dance!"
Red demon: "My stomach's bursting."
Blue demon: "I'm so drunk."
Momotaro took out his sword and leapt into the room. The demons, taken by surprise, brandished great metal clubs at him.

p. 22

Chief demon: "Who are you?"
Momotaro: "I am Momotaro, the best in Japan!"
Chief demon: "Go home, go home. We'll beat you with our clubs."
Momotaro: "Give back the treasure you stole from the villagers."
Dog: "I'll bite the demon's legs."

p. 23

Monkey: "I'll scratch the demon's faces."
Pheasant: "I'll peck the demon's heads."
As Momotaro, the dog, the monkey, and the pheasant had eaten the best millet dumplings in Japan, they were full of energy.

p. 24

Chief demon: "We're sorry. We'll give all the treasure back."
Red demon, blue demon: "We won't do wicked things any more. Please forgive us."
The demons were crying as they said how sorry they were.
Momotaro put the treasure on a cart, and went back to the village.
Villagers: "Ah, Momotaro's back. Hooray, hooray!"
Momotaro: "I'm home."
Old man: "Welcome home. Thank goodness, thank goodness."
Old woman: "Welcome home. Thank you so much for everything you've done."
Villagers: "Thank you, thank you. Momotaro, you really are the best in Japan."

THE END